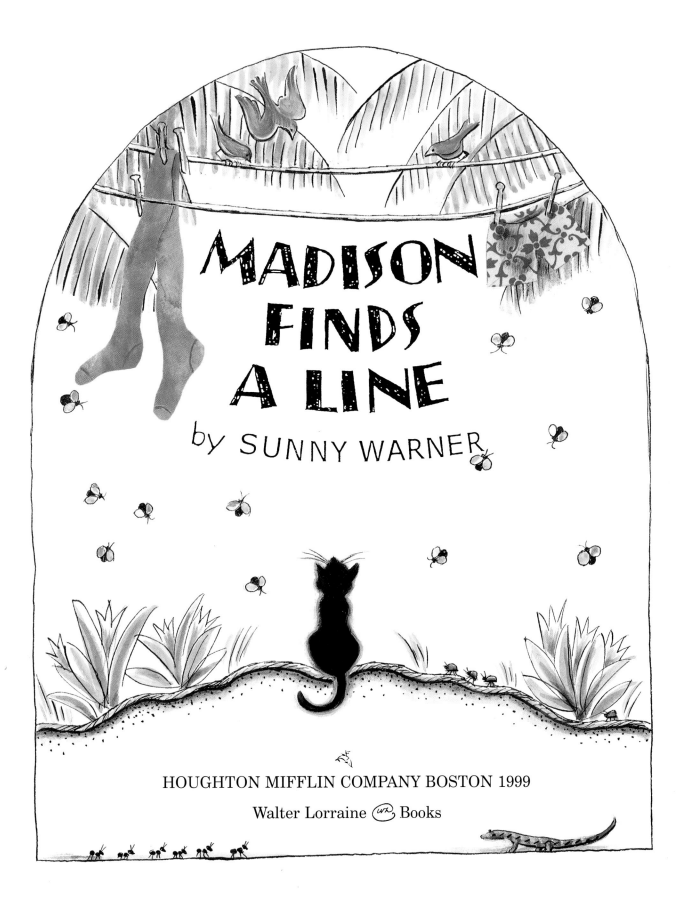

MADISON FINDS A LINE

by SUNNY WARNER

HOUGHTON MIFFLIN COMPANY BOSTON 1999

Walter Lorraine Books

This book is for Madison Roze, with love

Walter Lorraine ⓌⓁ Books

Copyright © 1999 by Sunny Warner

Library of Congress Cataloging-in-Publication Data

Warner, Sunny.
Madison finds a line / by Sunny Warner.
p. cm.
Summary: Madison and her cat Caspar follow a mysterious line
that takes them to a concert given by a band of bug musicians,
who join them in a watery adventure.
ISBN 0-395-88508-6
[1. Bands (Music) — Fiction. 2. Insects — Fiction. 3. Cats — Fiction.
4. Stories in rhyme.] I. Title.
PZ8.3.W2456Mad   1999
[E]—dc21   99-20696
                                              CIP

Printed in the United States of America
WOZ 10 9 8 7 6 5 4 3 2 1

One fine morning Madison was
playing in her yard.
She came upon a piece of rope
she gave some close regard.

"How curious, how interesting!
I'll follow it," she said,
and she set herself on a mission
to find out where it led.

"Hello, Caspar," she greeted her cat
with a friendly little song.
"I'm following this line I found.
Would you like to come along?"

"I don't mind," said the cat,
"that sounds just fine to me."

4

So they walked the line together,
   stepping carefully.

Then Madison stopped and looked ahead;
   "Do you hear music?" Madison said.

"I can't be certain, but I think it's coming . . . from behind this curtain."

Madison opened the curtain wide, and they stepped through.

On the other side,
    the line was not straight anymore.

Madison had   to zig   and zag   and dance   like a

toreador.

She did the shimmy-shammy rag
      (with Caspar dancing right along),
while they could hear the music playing
   and tiny voices raised in song.

They danced all pointy, and they danced all round.

And pretty soon they found
    with a RAZZMATAZZ!
the jitterbug band
    playing all that jazz.

"That's the
BASIN STREET
BLUES!
I know that song!"
said Madison
to Caspar,
and then she
sang along.

*"You'll never know
how much it means
just to be in New
Orleans, on Basin
Street, the street of
dreams . . ."*

When the music stopped
the drummer yelled,
"IT'S TIME FOR LUNCH,"
and they all scurried off
for something to munch.

"Thanks for the music,"
Madison called.
"Thanks for the concert in the park!
I really must be going home . . ."

It was getting very dark.

It grew so awfully dark and gray their line disappeared, and they lost their way. Then lightning flashed, and thunder roared; suddenly the rain just poured.

"Don't be scared," said Madison to Caspar, but she was getting scared herself, and began to run a whole lot faster.

Then all that water pouring down
    made puddles rise and flood the ground.
And still the water rose and rose . . .
    it reached her knees,

    it reached her nose.

"Great Grandma's goat! WE NEED A BOAT!"
    said Madison, paddling madly,
with Caspar clinging tight to her coat,
    and the two of them listing badly.

At this terrible moment,
awash in the foment,
their umbrella obligingly bobbed into sight.

When they clambered inside
it was pleasantly wide
(and they were glad that the timing was right).

As they rode in their craft,
    sighting fore, sighting aft,
they saw, all around them, and bobbing about,
    the bugs from the bug band, who sent up a shout.

"Ahoy!" called out Maddie, "Ahoy and what cheer!
It's not really a boat, but you're welcome in here!"

So into the bouncing umbrella they climbed,
and together they sailed along,
and everyone sang just as loud as they could
when the ladybugs struck up a song:

"Float, float, float your boat,

Gently down the stream,

Merrily, merrily, merrily, merrily,

...life is but a dream."

Then, "Land ho!"
shouted the dragonfly,
and they came aground,
and they said good-bye.

When Madison
saw the rainbow
   left by the rain,
they ran and ran
   to where it was,
and there they found
   their line again.

22

The sun shone bright, they loved the heat,
they danced the line with a salsa beat.

But soon
it grew colder;
they were
climbing a mountain.
They climbed
very high.
When they got to the top,
they came to a stop,
and Caspar let out a cry.

Then Madison saw
what was under his paw
and the two of them stood there to stare.
The line was flying straight across
a mile-high slice of air!

"Oh that's all right," said Madison,
"I've walked a rope before.
Though this one *might* be harder
since it isn't on the floor."

So taking the dare, the dauntless pair
    set out for the other side.
And in spite of their scare,
    with the greatest of care,
they crossed the dread divide.

When the line went swiftly down,

they danced all pointy
and they danced all round.

And then they were feeling
    as hungry as bears,
racing each other
    and leaping like hares.

Picturing wonderful things to eat,
they went faster
and faster
on hungry feet.

And soon they saw,
    to their great delight,
the big white curtain
    blowing bright.

Madison crowed,
    "I KNEW we could do it!"
and with one great leap,
    they flew right through it.

"MISSION ACCOMPLISHED!
        Hooray for that!"
Madison said
        to her brave little cat.

"And Caspar, look!"
        said she with a shout,
"Mama's laid
        the table out!
Just wait till I tell her
        what happened today
when we went out
        in the yard to play!"

THE END